Listen to the Silent Night

By
Dandi Daley Mackall

Paintings by
Steve Johnson & Lou Fancher

Dutton Children's Books ✳ An imprint of Penguin Group (USA) Inc.

Ellie and Cassie, this book is for you: Helen Isabella Hendren and Cassandra Eve Hendren

DDM

For our parents

SJ & LF

DUTTON CHILDREN'S BOOKS
A division of Penguin Young Readers Group

Published by the Penguin Group
Penguin Group (USA) Inc., 375 Hudson Street, New York, New York 10014, U.S.A.
Penguin Group (Canada), 90 Eglinton Avenue East, Suite 700, Toronto, Ontario, Canada M4P 2Y3
(a division of Pearson Penguin Canada Inc.)
Penguin Books Ltd, 80 Strand, London WC2R 0RL, England
Penguin Ireland, 25 St Stephen's Green, Dublin 2, Ireland (a division of Penguin Books Ltd)
Penguin Group (Australia), 250 Camberwell Road, Camberwell, Victoria 3124, Australia (a
division of Pearson Australia Group Pty Ltd)
Penguin Books India Pvt Ltd, 11 Community Centre, Panchsheel Park, New Delhi - 110 017, India
Penguin Group (NZ), 67 Apollo Drive, Rosedale, Auckland 0632, New Zealand (a division of Pearson New Zealand Ltd)
Penguin Books (South Africa) (Pty) Ltd, 24 Sturdee Avenue, Rosebank, Johannesburg 2196, South Africa
Penguin Books Ltd, Registered Offices: 80 Strand, London WC2R 0RL, England

CIP Data is available.

Published in the United States by Dutton Children's Books,
a division of Penguin Young Readers Group
345 Hudson Street, New York, New York 10014
www.penguin.com/youngreaders

Designed by Lou Fancher and Sara Lenton

Manufactured in China • First Edition
ISBN 978-0-525-42276-1
1 3 5 7 9 10 8 6 4 2

*I*n our hearts, find a silence in the middle of the noise,
With the bustling of our Christmas and the clattering of toys.
Help us slip into the silence, filled with hallelujah joys
On not such a silent night.

It was not such a silent night.
Hear the *who, who, who* as a night owl flew,
'Cross a winding trail where a cold wind blew.
Mary knew her time must be nearly due
For the Son who would set things right.

It was not such a silent night.
Hear the *flip, flap, flap* Joseph's sandals made.
Roman soldiers passed, and their horses neighed.
Mary rolled and bounced, while the donkey swayed
As she rode toward the Bethlehem light.

It was not such a silent night.
Hear the *oomph! oomph! oomph!* of the shoving game
Down in Bethlehem, where the faithful came,
As the growing crowds tried to stake their claim
At the inns on that festival night.

It was not such a silent night.

Hear the *rap*, *tap*, *tap* on the inn's big door.

Joseph begged for rooms, but there were no more.

Then they found a barn, just a hay-tossed floor,

Where they prayed and prepared for the night.

It was not such a silent night.

Hear the *moo! moo! moo!* of a cow or two.

And the rooster crowed, "Cock-a-doodle-doo!"

Mary settled in by this noisy crew,

Keeping watch for the dawning of light.

It was not such a silent night.

Hear the *swish, swish, swish* of the desert sand

As the camels raced toward a far-off land,

And the Wise Men rode with their gifts in hand

Toward the star that was brighter than bright.

It was not such a silent night.
Hear the *baa*, *baa*, *baa* of the sheep who crept
Up a hill so steep, where a moonbeam swept,
And the snoring sounds as the shepherds slept
Under skies that were starry and bright.

It was not such a silent night.
Hear the *flut-flut-flutter* of angel wings.
Hear the wondrous message the angel brings,
While a host of angels from heaven sings,
"Christ the King has been born this night!"

It was not such a silent night.

Hear the *whoosh, whoosh, whoosh* as the staffs waved free,

While the shepherds cried, "We must go and see!

The Messiah's here! Born for you and me!"

So they raced toward the glorious sight.

It was not such a silent night.

Mary *groaned* in pain, Joseph by her side.

Then a *shout* rang out—Baby Jesus cried!

So they held him close, filled with joy and pride.

A miraculous Christmas night!